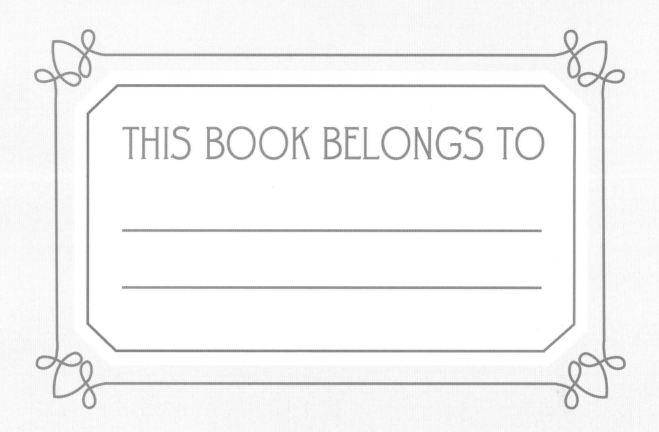

THIS BOOK BELONGS TO

_____

_____

THE
RAGGEDY
ANN

100TH ANNIVERSARY TREASURY

ADAPTED FROM STORIES BY JOHNNY GRUELLE
ILLUSTRATED BY JAN PALMER

LITTLE SIMON

New York   London   Toronto   Sydney   New Delhi

LITTLE SIMON

An imprint of Simon & Schuster Children's Publishing Division

1230 Avenue of the Americas, New York, New York 10020

Raggedy Ann and Andy and the Camel with the Wrinkled Knees copyright 1924 by P.F. Volland Co.; copyright renewed 1951 by Myrtle Gruelle; adaptation copyright © 1998 by Simon & Schuster, Inc.; illustrations copyright © 1998 by Simon & Schuster, Inc.

Raggedy Ann's Wishing Pebble copyright © 1925 by the P.F. Volland Company; adaptation copyright © 1999 by Simon & Schuster, Inc.; illustrations copyright © 1999 by Simon & Schuster, Inc.

Raggedy Ann and Rags copyright © 1929 by John B. Gruelle; copyright renewed 1956 by Myrtle Gruelle; adaptation copyright © 2002 by Simon & Schuster, Inc.; illustrations copyright © 2002 by Simon & Schuster, Inc.

How Raggedy Ann Got Her Candy Heart adaptation copyright © 1998 by Simon & Schuster, Inc.; illustrations copyright © 1998 by Simon & Schuster, Inc.

Raggedy Ann and Andy and the Nice Police Officer copyright © 1929 by The Johnny Gruelle Company; adaptation copyright © 1999 by Simon & Schuster, Inc.; illustrations copyright © 1999 by Simon & Schuster, Inc.

This Little Simon bind-up edition 2015

All rights reserved, including the right of reproduction in whole or in part in any form.

LITTLE SIMON is a registered trademark of Simon & Schuster, Inc., and associated colophon is a trademark of Simon & Schuster, Inc.

For information about special discounts for bulk purchases, please contact Simon & Schuster Special Sales at 1-866-506-1949 or business@simonandschuster.com.

The Simon & Schuster Speakers Bureau can bring authors to your live event. For more information or to book an event contact the Simon & Schuster Speakers Bureau at 1-866-248-3049 or visit our website at www.simonspeakers.com.

Manufactured in China 0317 SCP

10 9 8 7 6 5 4 3

ISBN 978-1-4814-4434-7

ISBN 978-1-4814-4532-0 (eBook)

These titles were previously published individually.

TABLE OF CONTENTS

HOW
RAGGEDY ANN
GOT HER CANDY HEART

One day Marcella
came into the nursery.
"You're invited to a tea party,"
she told the dolls.
"We can sit outside and watch
the men painting the house."

Marcella brought all the dolls outside.
They sat in red chairs at her table
under the old apple tree.
They drank lemonade with grape jelly in it,
which made it a beautiful lavender color.
They ate cream puffs and tiny
little cookies with powdered sugar.

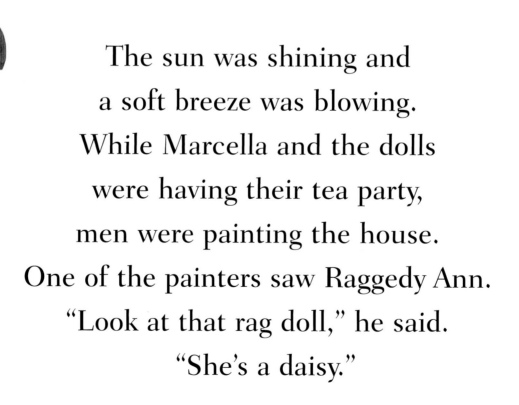

The sun was shining and
a soft breeze was blowing.
While Marcella and the dolls
were having their tea party,
men were painting the house.
One of the painters saw Raggedy Ann.
"Look at that rag doll," he said.
"She's a daisy."

Raggedy Ann didn't notice the painters, because she was watching some boys who were flying a kite. One boy lifted the kite above his head, while another held a ball of string. Suddenly, a breeze took the kite from the first boy.

The kite climbed high in the air. Then it fell down.

"It needs a longer tail!" one boy shouted.

"Let's tie Raggedy Ann to the tail!" Marcella suggested. "I know she would enjoy a trip way up in the sky."

The boys were delighted with this new idea. So Raggedy Ann was tied to the tail of the kite. Raggedy Ann was happy, too. She thought she might like to be up high.

This time the kite rose straight in the air, and Raggedy Ann was way, way up and far away. How Raggedy Ann enjoyed being up there! She could see for miles. The house and children were tiny, and her shoe-button eyes couldn't even spot the other dolls.

Just then there was a great puff of wind and Raggedy Ann heard a ripping sound. It was the rag that tied her to the kite.

Down below, Marcella was getting restless.
"Will you please pull the kite down now?" she asked the boys.
"I want Raggedy Ann."

The boys didn't want Raggedy Ann to come down. But the
wind puffed again and the rag tore.

Raggedy Ann went sailing through the air as the wind caught in her skirts. The kite began darting and swooping to the ground. It landed in the apple tree. And as the boys, Marcella, and all the other dolls watched, Raggedy Ann flew out of the sky and fell into a can of paint!

Marcella ran to her doll. Oily, white housepaint covered
Raggedy Ann's yarn hair and her shoe-button eyes. It covered
her pretty blue dress and her striped stockings. It soaked into
her cotton stuffing.

The nice painter who liked Raggedy Ann fished her out
of the paint can. "My goodness!" he said. He looked at Marcella.
"If you let me, I'll take her home with me. I'll clean her
up tonight and bring her back."

Marcella nodded. She was too upset to speak.

The painter wrapped Raggedy Ann in newspaper. Then he brought her home and washed her in a tub.

He put her feet in the clothes wringer, and his wife
turned the crank. It was hard work, but Raggedy Ann came
through the clothes wringer. She was flat as a pancake,
and so was her smile.

The painter hung Raggedy Ann on the clothesline, and he and his wife sat down to supper.

Raggedy Ann swung upside down on the clothesline. Even after the sun went down, it was still warm outside. She wasn't lonely, because the moon and the stars kept her company.

Just before dawn, a robin and his wife flew by. They asked
Raggedy Ann if they could have some of her yarn hair to line a
nest for their little babies. Raggedy Ann smiled at them.
They took yarn from her head and some of her cotton stuffing.

When the sun was all the way up and Raggedy Ann was quite dry and toasty warm, the painter unclipped her from the clothesline and brought her back inside.

He sewed new yarn on her hair. Then he took out the rest of her old stuffing and filled her full of fluffy new white cotton. "Don't sew her up yet," said his wife.

She pulled a paper bag from a cupboard, reached inside, and fished out a red candy heart. It had blue letters printed on it that said I LOVE YOU.

The painter took the heart from his wife. He poked it inside Raggedy Ann, just where her heart would be, and sewed her up like new. Then he said good-bye to his wife and went back to finish painting Marcella's family's house.

Marcella and the dolls had passed a sad night. They missed their friend and they wondered if they would see her again.

When the painter arrived, they were waiting under the apple tree. "Here she is," said the painter. "Fresh as a daisy." Marcella hugged Raggedy Ann. She smelled so good!

That night all the dolls arranged themselves around Raggedy
Ann in the nursery, and she told them about being washed and
put through the clothes wringer. She told them about Mama
and Papa Robin and about being dried and stuffed and made
just like new. Last of all, she told them about the candy heart
that read I LOVE YOU.

RAGGEDY ANN

AND RAGS

One clear, summer night, Raggedy Ann, Raggedy Andy, and Uncle Clem were sitting in front of the playhouse. Marcella had played outside with them that afternoon, and had been called into the house. Now the sun had gone down, and the evening shadows had turned everything a lovely purple. The little fireflies came up out of the grass and sailed high into the air.

"Who knows?" Raggedy Ann said in a whispery, cotton-soft voice. "Perhaps we may see the fairies."

"Oh! I wish we could," said Uncle Clem.

"*Shh!*" said Raggedy Andy very quietly. "What is that?" They heard something like a twig snapping near the orchard fence. The dolls waited.

The moon had risen, and now a tiny puppy dog came into sight. The puppy's fur was white with brown spots, and he had soft, black eyes. He trotted up to the dolls and sniffed each of them in turn.

"You are very small to be on your own at night," Raggedy Ann told the dog. "Where is your mama?"

The tiny puppy dog said nothing. He licked Raggedy Ann's face with his pink tongue, climbed into her lap and turned around, and fell asleep. Raggedy Ann and the other dolls sat quietly, watching the night and the fireflies and the puppy dog.

Bright and early the next morning, Marcella ran out to the playhouse. When she saw the dolls, she ran back to the house. "Daddy! Mama! Come quick!" she cried.

Mama and Daddy followed Marcella to where the dolls sat. Raggedy Ann held a tiny puppy dog on her lap, partly covered by her apron.

"Maybe the fairies brought him," Marcella said.

"I wonder where his mother is," said her daddy. "Well, we can't leave him out here."

Carefully, Marcella picked up the puppy dog and brought him into the kitchen. Her daddy followed with the dolls. Mama found a saucer of warm milk for the puppy, and he lapped it up hungrily.

"What are you going to call him?" Daddy asked.

"Raggedy Ann found him," Marcella said. "I shall call him Rags."

All that summer, Rags drank warm milk, and he grew bigger and stronger. He learned to bark, though he could never tell the dolls where he came from or who his mama was.

Marcella liked to dress Rags in a doll's cap and nightie. She fed him treats, and sometimes they played tug-of-war with an old stocking. Rags chewed Papa's socks until Mama found out and said, "Bad dog!" so sternly that Rags went to hide in the closet.

But he couldn't be downhearted, especially after one of Marcella's tea parties, when he would lick the crumbs from the dolls' faces. Every night at bedtime, Daddy would let Rags outside, and he would run around the house and bark. Then he would fall asleep in the garden, keeping one eye half-open for the rabbits.

Most nights, Marcella put the dolls to sleep in the nursery, but if she was called to an early supper, the dolls would stay outside. One evening in August, some of them were left on the beach. As soon as he was let outside, Rags ran around the house. He barked at the playhouse and at the stone wall by the beach. Then he joined the dolls near the water, where he barked and barked at the moon, wagging his stumpy tail.

"Mercy!" said Raggedy Ann. "What are you barking at?"

Rags said nothing, but trotted up to Raggedy Ann and licked her hand. She had to laugh, for she knew he just wanted to pretend he was taking good care of them all.

"Raggedy Ann, will you come sailing with me?" asked Squeakie. She was a new doll in the nursery, stuffed with wood and sawdust. She had found a flat board just the size for the two dolls, with a string tied to the front.

Raggedy Ann thought a sail was a fine idea, so she and Squeakie pushed the wood into the water and climbed on top. Gentle waves lapped at the board, and a sudden breeze pushed them away from the shore, where Raggedy Andy, Uncle Clem, and Cleety the clown were looking for hermit crabs, and Rags was barking at minnows in the shallow pools.

Raggedy Ann and Squeakie sat, arms around each other, looking at the silvery trail of the moon on the water. It was so peaceful, they didn't realize how far they had drifted, and none of their friends onshore noticed their absence. Not even Rags noticed, and he made it his business to notice everything!

"Goodness! What a noise!" Raggedy Andy exclaimed. Rags was barking furiously, running up and down at the edge of the water.

"Look!" Cleety said, pointing. "Raggedy Ann and Squeakie have gone sailing."

"They're awfully far out," said Uncle Clem. "Perhaps they need to be rescued."

"But how?" asked Raggedy Andy. "We can't swim, for our stuffing will be waterlogged if we try. No, Rags," he added, for Rags had flung himself into the water as if prepared to swim all the way out to the two sailors.

"I know!" Cleety said suddenly. "The steamboat. It runs very fast in the water."

Marcella had a little steamboat that she often brought down to the water, which ran by a little key that turned a paddle wheel. It lay not far away on the beach.

They all ran over to the steamboat and carried it to the water. But when they tried to climb on board, the little boat turned over and sank.

"This will never do," said Uncle Clem. "All of us except Cleety are too large to ride on the steamboat. Cleety will have to be engineer and captain and everything."

So Cleety the clown climbed onto the little steamboat, and Raggedy Andy and Uncle Clem waded out into the water and gave it a grand push. Rags barked and dashed into the water and back again, but Raggedy Andy took hold of his collar before he could plunge into deep water and swim alongside the boat. Cleety wound the key in the smokestack, and then he waved to his friends and guided the steamboat across the water.

Raggedy Andy and Uncle Clem and Rags walked back to the stone wall and sat down. The two dolls and the puppy watched as Cleety and the steamboat sped away across the silvery wake of the moon. Rags looked up at Raggedy Andy from time to time, as if to say, "I can swim out and help Cleety," but he kept still and didn't bark.

Cleety wound and wound the key, and the steamboat sailed through the water. A wild duck swooped down and was so startled by the sight of a clown on a little boat that it flew away, not even answering Cleety's question: "Have you seen two nice dolls drifting on a board?"

So Cleety sailed on and on.

Cleety circled around the bunches of swamp grass toward Peach Island. He had just about given up hope of finding the dolls when he heard Squeakie's voice, from far across the water, say, "What is that thing sailing out there, Raggedy Ann? It looks like a tiny ship."

Then Raggedy Ann said, "It *is* a tiny ship, Squeakie, and look! Cleety the clown is making it go."

So Cleety ran the little steamboat up to where Raggedy Ann sat upon the wooden board, holding Squeakie on her lap.

"My goodness!" said Raggedy Ann. "How glad we are to see you, Cleety. We have had a most delightful sail, but it would never do for us to drift out to sea."

"That's why I'm here," Cleety said. "Raggedy Andy and Uncle Clem and Rags would have come, but the little steamboat wouldn't hold them."

"Then we shall have to hug them when we are back onshore," said Squeakie. "And I intend to hug you, too!"

Cleety thought that would be very nice, and said so. Then he tied the board to the little steamboat, turned the key, and headed for shore.

The journey back was a slow one, for Raggedy Ann and Squeakie and the board were a heavy cargo, and Cleety had to rewind the key many times. As they neared the beach, they heard loud barking. Rags had spotted them, and he was running excitedly up and down at the edge of the water.

"Look!" said Raggedy Andy. He also had spotted the little steamboat and the two dolls on the board. He and Uncle Clem joined Rags by the water.

Rags couldn't wait another second. He jumped into the water and swam out to meet the sailors, almost upsetting the little steamboat with the waves he made.

"Now, Rags, please be careful," Raggedy Ann said. "We are glad to see you, but you must not sink us!"

So Rags swam behind the little steamboat and carefully placed his black nose against the board. He pushed the board and the steamboat toward the beach until Raggedy Andy and Uncle Clem could pull them the rest of the way.

Once onshore, Raggedy Ann and Squeakie gave Cleety big hugs for rescuing them, and then they hugged Raggedy Andy and Uncle Clem for good measure.

Rags ran around them in circles. He was so happy to see everyone back safe and sound! Then he shook himself all over.

"Stop, Rags," said Raggedy Ann. But she wasn't really angry. She sat, and Rags flopped down beside her. The other dolls sat in the sand nearby, and that was how Marcella found them in the morning.

"Oh, poor babies. You're all damp!" Marcella said. She gathered the dolls in her arms. "I must take you inside and feed you breakfast, or you will surely catch a chill." Raggedy Ann looked at Raggedy Andy, and their shoe-button eyes twinkled.

As for Rags, he ran around the house three times and then went to sleep in the garden, with one eye half-open for the rabbits.

RAGGEDY ANN
AND ANDY AND THE CAMEL WITH
THE WRINKLED KNEES

One day Raggedy Ann
and Andy were walking in
the deep, deep woods
when they met their friend,
the Camel with the
wrinkled knees.
The Camel's legs were so
wrinkled and soft
that he seemed almost to
fall every time he took a step.
"Wup!" Raggedy Andy said,
as he helped the Camel
sit down. "You almost fell over
that time."
"Indeed I did," said the Camel.
"My legs aren't what
they used to be."

Raggedy Ann tried to smooth out the wrinkles in the Camel's knees, but he smiled and said,

"That won't do a bit of good. When I was brand new, I had sticks inside each leg to keep them straight. After a few weeks the sticks poked through my legs, so the mother of the little boy who played with me pulled them out. Now my knees are saggy and soft, but I'm much more comfortable when I lie down."

Raggedy Ann felt her candy heart go *thump, thump,* for
she was glad to hear the Camel's story. "Maybe you can help
us," she said. "Last night we heard footsteps in the nursery.
Now our friend Babette, the French doll, is gone. We don't
know where she is."

The Camel scratched his head with his floppiest leg.
"Maybe I can help you," he said.

"I think I can find Babette," said the Camel, "if I cover my eyes with a hanky, and if I run backward to the place where I came from. You had better climb up and ride."

So Raggedy Ann and Andy climbed onto his soft flannel back. The Camel started walking slowly, then faster, until his wobbly, wrinkled legs were hitting the ground *clumpity, clumpity, clumpity* and he was running surprisingly fast.

After they had run along for ten minutes, they heard a *clip, clop,* and Raggedy Andy turned to see a funny old horse running toward them. The Camel stopped suddenly, and the horse ran straight into him. Raggedy Ann and Andy fell over the Camel's nose. The poor Camel's head was pushed flat into the ground, and his wrinkled neck was wrinkled up against his body.

The horse sat down on his back legs and sighed. "I'm so tired," he said. "I am old, and the least exercise wears me out."

Raggedy Ann and Andy were busy pulling the Camel's head back into shape and removing the hanky from his eyes so he could see. "We were running to find our friend Babette," said Raggedy Ann. "We think she was kidnapped."

"I am running away from pirates," said the tired old horse. "Maybe they have your friend." He pointed to a large tent not far away.

Very, very quietly, the dolls, the horse, and the Camel crept
up to the tent. They peeked into a small hole. Inside were
twelve large pirates with mustaches. And in the corner, all
alone, stood Babette.

"Listen," Raggedy Ann whispered.

"Ha!" said one pirate. "I am the bravest pirate around here."

"We are all the bravest," said all of the other pirates.

"They'll all be fighting in a few minutes," said Raggedy Andy.

Then Raggedy Andy picked up a small stone, no bigger than a pea. He threw it softly into the tent, so it bounced off one pirate's shoe.

"Ow!" the pirate howled. "Who hit me?"

Raggedy Andy threw another tiny pebble, and suddenly the pirates decided that it would be safer outside the tent. There was a jam at the doorway, and the pirates all fell in a tangle of arms, legs, and heads, pulling the tent down with them.

Raggedy Ann quickly reached under the fallen tent and found Babette. She was unhurt and very happy to see her friends.

The tired old horse turned to the pirates, who had just stopped fighting. "Now you must promise to reform and not be pirates and kidnappers anymore. And then I'll give you each a lollipop." He knew that the pirates had nothing to eat all day but bread and butter and pickles. He held twelve lollipops high, so the pirates could not reach them.

"I'll stop being a pirate and be a plumber," cried one pirate.

"I'll stop and go into the garage business," another pirate shouted.

When all the pirates had said "Cross my heart!" the tired old horse gave them each a lollipop. Then the three dolls, the Camel, the horse, and the pirates all climbed into the pirates' flying boat, and it jumped into the sky and sped away.

Soon the boat came to rest in the dolls' backyard. Raggedy Ann, Raggedy Andy, and Babette said good-bye to their friends and crept into their playroom, where all the other dolls were sound asleep. They climbed into their beds, bounced up and down once, and smiled. Then they fell asleep, too.

RAGGEDY ANN'S
WISHING PEBBLE

Raggedy Ann and Andy

were rag dolls stuffed with nice white
cotton. They had bright shoe-button
eyes and happy smiles painted on
their rag faces. One day they were
poking about by the Looking Glass
Brook when Raggedy Andy held up
a round white pebble. "Do you think
this is a wishing pebble?" he asked.

"I have no idea," said Raggedy Ann.
"Let's make a wish."

"Why don't we wish for something
for our friends, the Muskrats?"
Raggedy Andy asked. "They always
give us Muskrat bread and butter
when we visit."

Raggedy Ann and Andy both squeezed the pebble as hard as they could and Raggedy Ann said, "I wish the Muskrats had a magic soda-water fountain right in their living room." They agreed that it was a good wish, and then they went to sleep in the sun.

The dolls were awakened a little later by Freddy Fieldmouse.

"There's a magic soda-water fountain in the Muskrats' home," he exclaimed. "They're inviting everyone for ice-cream sodas!" He scampered off.

"That means the wishing pebble was real!" Raggedy Ann said. "Let's go see the fountain." She buried the pebble in the sand before heading off to the Muskrats.

Raggedy Ann and Andy found a crowd of animals at the Muskrats' home, all drinking sodas. When the dolls told them about the magic wishing pebble, Mister and Missus Muskrat thanked them for their kindness. Missus Muskrat snipped a hole in the center of each doll's mouth, so they could try the sodas for themselves.

"Whee!" Raggedy Ann cried, after she and Andy drank fifteen ice-cream sodas. "I don't believe I can drink another one. Let's go find the wishing pebble that I buried in the sand."

"That's a fine idea," cried Missus Muskrat. She and the other animals and the dolls ran to the brook. They hunted in the loose sand on the bank, but they couldn't find the wishing pebble.

Mister Muskrat had stayed home to wash the soda glasses, but now he ran to join them. "It's gone!" he cried. "The magic fountain just disappeared!"

"Of course it's gone," a voice sounded from across the brook.

"Who is that?" Raggedy Andy shouted.

"Ha! Ha!" said the voice. "I saw where Raggedy Ann buried the wishing pebble. I took it and wished the magic soda fountain would disappear from the Muskrats' house. Now I have the fountain and the wishing pebble too!"

Missus Muskrat couldn't keep from crying. "I had planned on all of our friends helping themselves to ice-cream sodas from the magic fountain," she sobbed.

Mister Muskrat wiped his eyes. "It's so nice to have a cold ice-cream soda on a hot day."

"Don't cry," said Raggedy Ann. "We'll get the pebble back."

While the animals were comforting the Muskrats, Raggedy Ann and Andy slipped away and crossed the brook. They got a little wet, but they soon dried in the sunshine.

"Do you know what?" asked Raggedy Ann. "I'll bet whoever has the wishing pebble can't make the fountain work because he is so unkind."

"Stop talking about me!" said the mysterious voice. "I'll bet you two old rag dolls are the reason my sodas taste like burnt candy!"

Raggedy Ann and Andy ignored the voice and walked along the bank, looking for clues to the missing pebble. Just as they passed under a large tree, a big checkered tablecloth fell down on top of their heads. Before they could untangle themselves, their feet were tied together by a little man with thin legs and a long nose. And when he spoke, they recognized the mysterious voice. It was Minky, who was known by everyone for his tricks and pranks.

"Ha!" said Minky. "I'm not letting you go until you tell me how to use the wishing pebble. I need a new magic fountain with soda that tastes sweet!"

"Selfish man!" Raggedy Ann laughed at Minky. "The wishing pebble only brings good things when you wish for something nice for others."

Suddenly Minky let out a howl and fell onto the grass. "Something is biting me!" Tears streamed down his face as he got to his feet and ran away.

"There!" Clifton Crawdad appeared suddenly, rubbing his big claws together. "Minky filled my doorway with mud one day, and it took me a long time to clean it out. Now I've pinched him with my claws, so we're even."

He quickly untied the dolls.

"Thank you!" said Raggedy Andy. "We'd better find Minky."

"It's no trouble," Clifton said, and burrowed back into his mud house.

Raggedy Ann and Andy crossed the brook again and ran into Winnie
Woodchuck.

"What happened?" she asked. "You're soaking wet! Come inside this
minute." She hustled Raggedy Ann and Andy inside their home, and
Walter Woodchuck made them comfortable in front of the crackly fire.
They sat and drank licorice tea and ate Woodchuck cookies, which are
made from twigs and hazelnuts.

Suddenly the door burst open and Minky stomped inside. "Give me
those cookies!" he shouted.

"Now you march right out, Mister Minky!" said Winnie Woodchuck.
"You are very rude."

But before he could leave, Raggedy Andy said, "That pebble belongs to us!" He grabbed Minky by his jacket.

"Stop, Andy!" cried Raggedy Ann. "Now *you're* being mean. And when you're unkind, the wishing pebble won't work properly. That's why Minky's sodas aren't sweet." Raggedy Andy let go of Minky, and the little man ran out the door.

It was quiet for a minute, then Raggedy Ann's shoe-button eyes twinkled and she whispered, "I'll bet Minky is listening outside the window."

Walter Woodchuck smiled. "Let's go outside and look for the magic lollipop garden," he said loudly. "Someone told me it's growing in the grass by the brook."

The Woodchucks and dolls snuck down to the brook, where Minky was crawling in the long grass. "What are you looking for?" asked Raggedy Ann.

"You know perfectly well!" Minky replied angrily. "Go away. The magic lollipops are mine!" Then he slipped in the muddy grass and fell into the deepest part of the brook.

Minky couldn't swim very well, so Raggedy Ann held out a long stick to him and pulled him ashore. "Why are you so kind when I was mean to you?" the little man asked. Water dripped from his jacket and long nose. "It was wrong of me to take your lovely wishing pebble. It's just that none of the animals like me, so I wanted to play a trick on them." He sniffed loudly.

Raggedy Ann smiled. "Don't feel sad, Minky," she said. She held out the wishing pebble, which had fallen from Minky's pocket. "I just wished the soda fountain was back at the Muskrats. And I wished for a lollipop garden in your backyard. I'll bet if you bring the Muskrats some lollipops, they'll give you a soda and let you stay for dinner. They're really very nice once you get to know them."

While Minky went to look for his new lollipop garden, Raggedy Ann and Andy decided to try one last soda at the Muskrats' house. On their way home they passed Minky digging in his garden. They waved good-bye, and then left to join their friends in the nursery.

RAGGEDY ANN

AND ANDY AND THE NICE
POLICE OFFICER

It was a lovely day in June. The birds were singing, the bees were buzzing, and the air was filled with the perfume of flowers. Raggedy Andy took Raggedy Ann's hand and they set off into the deep, deep woods in search of adventure. They found a cool, green path that they had never seen before, and they soon arrived in a clearing.

"Boo-hoo, Boo-hoo."

"Listen," said Raggedy Andy. "Someone is crying." He pointed to a pretty little house with a red roof and flowers growing in the yard. A nice-looking policeman sat on the front step, sobbing into his hands.

Raggedy Ann said, "Let's see if we can help."

When the policeman saw the two rag dolls, he sobbed louder than ever.

"Mercy me," Raggedy Ann said. "Why are you crying so, Mr. Police Officer?"

"Oh, it is too sad," he replied. "I found a note on my front door that said, 'Please arrest Mr. Hooligooly.' I have never arrested anyone before!"

"Perhaps someone is angry with Mr. Hooligooly and would like to get him into trouble," Raggedy Ann mused. "Maybe he hasn't done anything wrong."

THE HOOLIGOOLYS

"That is true," the police officer said. A smile came to his face as Raggedy Ann dried the last of his tears.

"Let's go see Mr. Hooligooly," she suggested.

When they reached the front steps of the Hooligooly house, the policeman caught Raggedy Ann's arm. "I don't want to arrest Mr. Hooligooly today," he pleaded. "Let's go back to my house."

"I'll knock on the door," said Raggedy Andy. He wiggled his shoe-button eyes and knocked once, twice, then a third time.

"Who's there?" called Mr. Hooligooly.

"You see! Now you have done it," the policeman wailed. He would have run home if Raggedy Ann had not held on to his coattails.

"This nice police officer is here to arrest you," explained Raggedy Andy.

"Maybe you'd better come in," Mr. Hooligooly said politely.

Raggedy Ann liked the Hooligoolys the minute she saw them. They had cheery smiles and merry twinkles in their eyes.

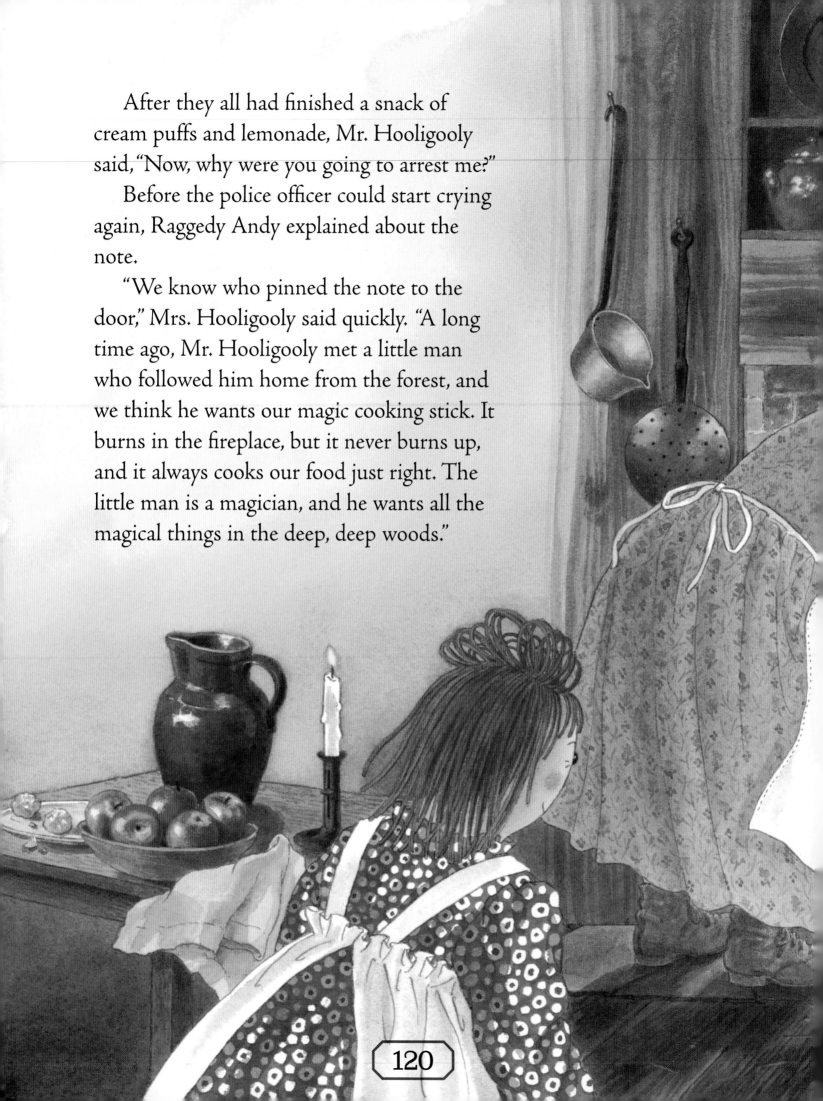

After they all had finished a snack of cream puffs and lemonade, Mr. Hooligooly said, "Now, why were you going to arrest me?"

Before the police officer could start crying again, Raggedy Andy explained about the note.

"We know who pinned the note to the door," Mrs. Hooligooly said quickly. "A long time ago, Mr. Hooligooly met a little man who followed him home from the forest, and we think he wants our magic cooking stick. It burns in the fireplace, but it never burns up, and it always cooks our food just right. The little man is a magician, and he wants all the magical things in the deep, deep woods."

"Let's go to the magician's house and tell him he can't behave that way," Raggedy Andy suggested.

Mr. Hooligooly said, "What a good idea." They left the Hooligoolys' house with the nice police officer, who would rather have stayed home and helped Mrs. Hooligooly cook dinner. Raggedy Ann stayed with Mrs. Hooligooly, for she was very curious about the magic cooking stick.

At the magician's house, Raggedy Andy climbed up on the roof and disappeared down the chimney. He planned to unlock the door from the inside. When he didn't reappear, Mr. Hooligooly knocked on the door.

"Run home to your mama," called the magician. "I'm holding your friend prisoner."

"We have come to arrest you," said the nice police officer bravely.

Suddenly the door opened, and two pancakes rolled out and landed in front of Mr. Hooligooly and the policeman.

Now they had no idea that these were magic pancakes. For just a moment, they forgot all about their friend Raggedy Andy.

"It is just dandy to have pancakes roll right into our laps," said the nice police officer.

"It surely is," said Mr. Hooligooly, as he took a bite of his pancake.

As soon as Mr. Hooligooly and the policeman bit into their pancakes, they turned into little squealy pigs and . . .

ran
right
home
to Mrs. Hooligooly.

Raggedy Ann and Mrs. Hooligooly were making lovely doughnuts and cream pies when two little squealy pigs ran into the house. The pigs were dressed in Mr. Hooligooly's and the police officer's clothes.

"Mercy me!" said Mrs. Hooligooly, who was about to shoo the pigs outside with her broom.

"Stop, Mrs. Hooligooly," cried Raggedy Ann. "Look at their clothes!
That's Mr. Hooligooly and the police officer!"

Raggedy Ann quickly closed the door. She saw a piece of a pancake sliding out of one pig's pocket. After breaking the pancake into tiny pieces, Raggedy Ann sprinkled it on top of a whipped-cream pie. She opened the front door and put the delicious-looking pie on the steps. Then she closed the door again.

In just a minute, Raggedy Ann opened the door, and a third little pig ran inside the house, dressed in the magician's clothes. "There!" said Raggedy Ann. "I knew the magician would be lurking outside. I gave him some of his own medicine."

"But how do we change them back?" said Mrs. Hooligooly. "I don't like to have pigs in my parlor, even if one of them is my husband. And I'm sure they don't enjoy being pigs."

"If we go to the magician's house, we can hunt through his magic books and find out how to change them back," Raggedy Ann replied. "Do you want to come with us?" she asked the pigs.

All three pigs squealed so loudly that Mrs. Hooligooly held her hands over her ears. Raggedy Ann locked the magician pig in the cellar. Then she and Mrs. Hooligooly led the other two pigs to the magician's house.

The magician had left Raggedy Andy hanging on a hook by the fireplace. This didn't hurt his soft rag body, but he wished he could help his friends. While Raggedy Ann set him loose, Mrs. Hooligooly found the magician's red book on the kitchen table. She and Raggedy Ann read a magic spell from the book and changed the police officer and Mr. Hooligooly back into themselves.

"My goodness!" said Mr. Hooligooly. "I will never eat another pancake that appears out of nowhere." The friends brought the squealy magician pig to jail. Then Raggedy Ann said the spell that changed him back into a magician.

"You'll stay here until you say you're sorry," Raggedy Andy told the magician. "Our friend, the police officer, will stop by after dinner and look in on you." Then Raggedy Ann and Raggedy Andy, the Hooligoolys, and the nice police officer left the jail and went back to the house, where they cooked a delicious turkey dinner with the magic cooking stick.

After dinner, Raggedy Ann and Raggedy Andy went with the policeman to the jail, where they found the magician looking very sad. "I'm sorry," he said. "I used to be a grocer, until I found the magic book. Then I became very greedy and wanted everything that was magic. Now I just want to have friends again."

Raggedy Ann and Raggedy Andy looked at each other, and their shoe-button eyes twinkled with happiness.

"We are very glad," Raggedy Ann said, "for there is nothing that brings such happiness as friendship. We will let you go home and keep the magic book, as long as you wish for lovely things for others. What better way to make new friends!"

The magician promised he would, and the nice police officer let him out of jail. They all said good night, and the two rag dolls went home to their friends in the nursery.

THE HISTORY OF
RAGGEDY ANN

One day, a little girl named Marcella discovered an old rag doll in her attic. Because Marcella was often ill and had to spend much of her time at home, her father, a writer named Johnny Gruelle, looked for ways to keep her entertained. He was inspired by Marcella's rag doll, which had bright shoe-button eyes and red yarn hair. The doll became known as Raggedy Ann.

Knowing how much Marcella adored Raggedy Ann, Johnny Gruelle wrote stories about the doll. He later collected the stories he had written for Marcella and published them in a series of books. He gave Raggedy Ann a brother, Raggedy Andy, and over the years the two rag dolls acquired many friends.

Raggedy Ann has been an important part of Americana for more than a century, as well as a treasured friend to many generations of readers. After all, she is much more than a rag doll—she is a symbol of caring and love, of compassion and generosity. Her magical world is one that promises to delight children of all ages for years to come.